Dark and Full of Secrets

Clarion Books
Ticknor & Fields, a Houghton Mifflin Company
Text copyright © 1984 by Carol Carrick
Illustrations copyright © 1984 by Donald Carrick

Library of Congress Cataloging in Publication Data
Carrick, Carol.
Dark and full of secrets.

Summary: Christopher drifts too far away from shore
while snorkeling in the pond, then panics when he can't
touch bottom. His dog comes to his rescue.
[1. Ponds—Fiction.   2. Skin diving—Fiction.
3. Dogs—Fiction]   I. Carrick, Donald, ill.   II. Title.
PZ7.C2344Dar   1984   [E]   83-21017
PA ISBN 0-89919-536-9   ISBN 0-89919-271-8

Y 10 9 8 7 6 5 4 3

Dark and Full of Secrets

by CAROL CARRICK pictures by DONALD CARRICK

Clarion Books / Ticknor & Fields / New York

Early morning mist rose from the pond like steam from a witch's brew. Christopher's father held the canoe steady. Just as Christopher was climbing in, his dog Ben jumped in with him, making the boat rock.

"Ben!" Christopher yelled, pushing the dog out.

"Home, Ben! Go home!" his father ordered, pointing toward the house. Ben slunk away.

"Today will be a scorcher," Christopher's father said as they pushed off. "A good day for swimming."

"I don't like to go in the pond," said Christopher. "There are *things* in there and the bottom is all mucky."

It wasn't that Christopher didn't like swimming. In the ocean the waves rose clear green like glass and, when they broke over him, the sudsy foam made him tingle. But the pond was dark and full of secrets.

Christopher was startled when some lily pads scraped the bottom of the canoe. His father laughed at the look on his face.
"Did you think that was a sea monster?" he asked.
Christopher didn't like being laughed at.

"There *could* be one," he said.

After the paddle was over, Christopher's father went to the store. He came back with a mask and a snorkel for each of them and brought them down to the beach in front of their house.

"You're only afraid of the pond because it's a mystery to you," his father said. "Wait till you see what's down there."

"I'm not afraid. I just don't like it," Christopher grumbled. But he was excited about trying the mask.

His father showed him how to put it on and how to breathe through his mouth with the snorkel. Christopher floated on his stomach to look through the window of the mask. Ahead he could see his father's swimming feet.

Christopher followed. Away from the beach the bottom was muddy. His father motioned to him to be still and lifted a rock. Under it was a crayfish. Christopher reached out to pick it up and the crayfish shot backward.

He was chasing after it when an explosion of water splashed over his back. Then four furry legs churned the water ahead of him. Ben never wanted to be left behind. Christopher stood up and splashed the dog, who was swimming around them in circles.

"I'll *never* find that crayfish now!" Christopher said.

"I'm hungry anyway," his father answered. "Let's have some lunch."

After lunch his father read a newspaper on the porch, but Christopher wanted to hunt for another crayfish. As he waded in, a turtle slipped off a log into the water, making a tiny splash. Maybe he could catch it. Christopher quickly put on the mask and circled the log, but the turtle was gone.

Christopher paddled among the rocks where crayfish might be hiding. Ahead of him a school of tiny fish hung together like the mobile in his classroom. They turned, swam and turned together, as though blown by a breeze.

Farther along shore the pond was deeper, and spooky. Cedar trees had drowned and fallen into the water, sinking like ancient ships.

Christopher almost missed seeing the big bass because it was so still. The fish was resting in the shade of an overhanging tree.

Christopher stopped moving. He even tried to stop breathing. Then, with a delicate sweep of its tail, the bass swam off. Christopher followed with slow strokes until the fish disappeared in the gloom. His heart pounded with excitement. It was one of the biggest fish he had ever seen. Wait till he told his dad!

Now Christopher floated above a meadow of waving plants. He was beginning to feel part of the underwater world. His breath snored through the breathing tube. The ripples rocked his body. Soon Christopher was almost lulled to sleep.

But water had gradually seeped into his mask. When Christopher stood up to empty it, water closed over his head. His feet felt for the bottom. It wasn't there! He had drifted out too far. Frantic, Christopher tried to drain his mask and tread water at the same time, but he kept sinking.

He started to paddle toward shore. Something scratched his foot. Was it the big fish? He gasped in surprise, filling his mouth and his mouthpiece with water so he couldn't breathe.

The mask was fogged up. He couldn't see what was in the water with him. Maybe it was only a floating branch, but Christopher had panicked. He struggled and pulled off the mask, sinking again. He clawed his way to the surface, panting for air. Now there was water in his eyes.

"Dad!" he called, but the water gurgled in his throat. Then near his ear he heard a loud puffing. It was Ben!

Christopher managed to grab the dog's long tail and hung on. Ben swam away, towing Christopher behind. As soon as he could touch bottom, Christopher let go.

His father was standing by the water's edge. "You shouldn't be out that far alone," he called. But then he teased, "The sea monster might get you."

Christopher had to catch his breath. Water in his throat made him cough and his legs were wobbly. He stretched out on the warm sand as if he would never move again.

Christopher's father was concerned. "Are you okay?" he asked.

"Sure," Christopher answered, but he didn't sound so sure. "I did get out a little too far," he admitted.

But when he remembered all he had seen, he sat up. "Dad, it was great! It was like being a fish myself. And I saw the biggest lake bass in the whole world. I was *that* close." Christopher measured with his hands.

Before sunset, the whole family went for a canoe ride. This time Ben came along.

The pond was like a dark mirror, reflecting puffs of pale cloud. And like a mirror, Christopher couldn't see through it. But beyond that dark surface he knew there was a crayfish that swam backward, a turtle that liked to sun itself, and a bass that maybe no one else had ever seen.